NIGHTSONG

NIGHTSONG

THE LEGEND OF ORPHEUS AND EURYDICE

MICHAEL CADNUM

ORCHARD BOOKS ✳ SCHOLASTIC INC.

New York

Library of Congress Cataloging-in-Publication Data
Cadnum, Michael. Nightsong : the legend of Orpheus
and Eurydice / Michael Cadnum. – 1st ed. • p. cm.
Summary: Expands on the myth of Orpheus, a young
poet and musician who undertakes a terrifying journey to ask the ruler of the Underworld to return
the princess Eurydice, his beloved bride, after she is
killed by a venomous serpent. ISBN 0-439-54535-8
1. Orpheus (Greek mythology) – Juvenile fiction.
2. Eurydice (Greek mythology) – Juvenile fiction.
3. Mythology, Greek – Juvenile fiction. [1. Orpheus
(Greek mythology) – Fiction. 2. Eurydice (Greek
mythology) – Fiction. 3. Mythology, Greek – Fiction.]
I. Title: Legend of Orpheus and Eurydice. I. Title.
PZ7.C11724Nig 2006 [Fic] – dc22 2006000711
10 9 8 7 6 5 4 3 2 1   06 07 08 09 10
Printed in the U.S.A.   37 • Reinforced Binding for
Library Use • First edition, November 2006 The text
type was set in 19-point Post mediaeval. Book design by
Kristina Albertson

FOR SHERINA,
WITH ENDURING THANKS TO IRIS

STRETCHING

AMONG THE PEAR TREES

SILENT DEER

NIGHTSONG

1

ONE

ORPHEUS PAUSED beside the river.

The angry current churned, too hard and deep for an easy crossing, the cold white water surging through the black stones.

Once again he heard the troubling wail in the distance.

"Are you sure this is a safe place to cross, Prince Orpheus?" asked Biton, his young servant, making every effort to disguise his anxiety.

"I had heard it was a peaceful waterway, Biton," replied Orpheus, trying to sound reassuring. "But now that I look at it, I have my doubts."

It was a day when the approach of spring was still merely a hint in the sunlight. The two travelers had nearly reached their destination, the land where King Lycomede ruled with his daughter the princess Eurydice. Orpheus had sent no advance notice of his visit, but he expected a warm welcome. Monarch and shepherd alike were always glad to play host to the famous singer, and for his own part the poet was eager to set eyes on the princess, who was said to possess an ardent love of music – and a magical beauty.

"Let's wander down the river for a while," suggested Biton. "No doubt some strong-armed ferryman will offer his services."

Orpheus was tall and sturdily built, with hair the color of amber, but he had no great faith in his own physical powers when it came to such a violent flood. The poet cocked his head, listening for the distant cry – and heard it again, faint but persistent.

"Do you hear it, too, Biton?" asked Orpheus.

"I was hoping I was mistaken," the young servant responded regretfully. "To my ear, I'm afraid it sounds very much like a crying baby."

Vultures circled a rocky knoll not far up the hillside beyond the river. With each approach, the winged scavengers came closer to a tiny being apparently abandoned there, at the foot of a great ash tree.

"Look there, master, upriver!" said Biton excitedly. "A herd of goats is already halfway across. If goats can make it through the water, then surely we will find our footing!"

"Those aren't goats, Biton," said Orpheus grimly. He lifted his legendary silver lyre over his head, and waded out into the seething river.

Indeed, the poet thought, the animals in question were not anything like goats. They were a pack of wild dogs fighting hungrily to swim the current, no doubt attracted by the human infant's wail. Once there, Orpheus feared, the creatures would make quick work of the baby, and have the ferocity besides to fight over the scraps.

Orpheus sang out a prayer, that the river god might ease the tumbling waters just long enough for a poet and his trusted attendant to reach the opposite bank. He was the most famous singer in the world; his mother was one of the Muses – Calliope, the goddess of epic poetry – and his father was the mortal king Oeagrus of Thrace.

The Muses were daughters of Jupiter, and the nine of them empowered human talent in music, dance, and song. No poet but Orpheus could claim to be the offspring of such an immortal.

And it did seem that at the sound of the poet's song, the river relented in its brutal torrent — just slightly.

"Be careful, master!" called Biton, already far behind.

The poet had rescued Biton some years before, saving him from drowning in a sudden freshet in Rodos — a dry, rocky stream-bed had filled with a flash flood during a summer storm. Orpheus had given the orphan the affectionate name for an ox, because the boy was so strong, and even-tempered as well.

The poet reached the midpoint, where the river was deepest. The water spun, gathering around him, surrounding him with power that had been, until hours ago, snow on one of the mountains. Upriver, the pack of wild dogs was halfway across as well, struggling but making headway.

Orpheus lifted his voice again, in one of his favorite songs, the story of the many rivers falling out of the sky, flung by the hand of Jupiter. It was a beautiful, soothing tune, and it was wise to remind the river god that, for all his thunder and foam, he was subject to the pleasure of the sky.

Beyond, the vultures circled, ever closer to the tiny human being.

It was an old practice among farm laborers, when sharp poverty made it impossible to feed yet another mouth: An unwanted new-born was left alone, out under the heavens. There the Fates could determine the infant's future, although the poet knew that many such babies lost their lives. Like many before him, Orpheus was often troubled by the flinty ways of gods and men.

At last Orpheus reached the dry, white pebbles of the opposite bank.

He ran as hard as he was able, through brambles and winter-bare bushes, his strong legs driving upslope.

Not far downhill the pack of wild dogs shook dazzling moisture into the sunlight. And then they resumed their course, tumbling over one another in their eagerness.

Orpheus was nearly there, a stitch in his side, the muscles of his long legs burning.

He set down his lyre, and knelt, breathing hard.

The blue-black wings of the carrion birds swept upward, retreating awkwardly and reluctantly as the poet gathered the wailing infant, wrapped in rough-spun wool, into his arms.

Orpheus took a deep breath, and sang the first words of the old lullaby, "Hush, dear one, the friendly sun is high."

The infant stirred, a baby girl not more than a week or two old.

She gave a kick, and gazed up into the poet's smile. She cried no longer, and as the poet gave voice to the time-honored verse – the winds at peace with Apollo, lord of the sun – the infant grew calm.

But within moments the dogs were upon them.

TWO

THE PACK closed in.

The lead dog drew so near that Orpheus could feel the warmth from the feral body and smell his rank, hot breath.

He was a thickset brute, larger and less famished in appearance than the rest, with a square snout and fine golden fangs. An old, white scar along his spine showed where a shepherd's barbed arrow had broken off some summers ago. The dog had intent, silver-colored eyes, and uttered a rumbling growl.

The poet was afraid. Not so much for himself, but for the infant. And there was plenty of unease left over for him to consider his own flesh and bone, too. The wet, gaunt animals had spent a bleak winter, by the looks of them, and the poet felt a twinge of compassion for their empty bellies.

But he was not so frightened that he failed to remember the power of song.

"The divine Apollo's golden blessing on all of you," sang Orpheus, a friendly verse of greeting.

White Scar answered with a deeper growl.

"This baby is safe with me, my dear friend," sang Orpheus, an improvised air with a sweet melody that disguised the poet's growing anxiety.

The throng of hungry animals urged White Scar from behind, shouldering and slavering, but the big animal resisted, suspicion and wonder, perhaps, keeping him where he was for a few moments more.

Orpheus reached up, and placed the infant in a fork of the ancient ash tree, its branches leafless this chilly day. Some people believed that Diana, the goddess of the hunt, favored such venerable trees, and the poet was thankful for the old tree's sheltering limbs.

Then the young man hefted the shining lyre from the ground, and settled the gleaming musical instrument into the crook of his arm. His fingers were stiff and cold from the river crossing. Nevertheless, he began to play well, lifting his voice in a poem about Persephone.

It was the story of the graceful mortal woman kidnapped by the lord of the underworld. Some people believed that the arrival of spring flowers was a sign that Persephone was returning to the land of the daylight, bringing new life. Others held that enigmatic Pluto was a jealous lord, and released his wife into the upper world but rarely. Orpheus sang of how Persephone, exiled among the colorless shades of once living people, fondly remembered the creatures of daylight.

She was fond of the hunting animals, too, the poet sang – like the wild dog White Scar, with his fine teeth. The verses told of Persephone's regret that she could not enjoy the company of such hardy animals, imprisoned as she was in the dark-steeped realm of the dead.

Orpheus closed his eyes, and sang of Persephone's passion for all living things.

When his poem was done, Orpheus opened his eyes – and beheld only empty hillside where the dogs had been.

"They left!" panted Biton, hurrying up and brandishing his staff. "And it's a good thing for them, too," he added. "By Hercules, master, I'll kill any dog that so much as snaps at you!"

THREE

"I DO BELIEVE it's him!" whispered the farmer to his wife, eyeing Orpheus's lyre. "Yes, I'm sure it's the poet!"

Servants peered through the gate, and then hurried off to obey their master's orders.

"We have mare's milk and cow's cheese, Prince Orpheus," offered the landowner. "Soft-baked bread, if you please, and the sweetest olive oil under the sky."

Orpheus told Biton to pay the farmer with the best, bright-minted Lydian silver.

"This is far too generous!" said the farmer with a laugh – closing his hand tightly around the precious metal. "If bread and cheese will not please you, is there anything else I can get for the son of the immortal muse?"

He asked eagerly – but with a trace of caution, too.

Orpheus glanced around at the sleek geese and fat cows. This well-fed farmer's own children – three of them – gathered behind their father, too shy to speak.

The infant in the poet's arms made a tiny bleat – a sound very much like the young goats in a nearby pen – and squirmed hungrily. Along the path, Orpheus's repertoire of sweet-sounding refrains had reassured the infant, but even the finest song fell short of being food.

"Some repast for this baby, if you please," said Orpheus. "And directions, if you would be so kind," added the poet with a smile, "to the court of the king."

"I shall call this child Melia," said Orpheus later that day as the two travelers continued into the woods. *Ash tree*. "Because of the branches that offered her welcome – and so that Diana might always protect her."

The baby was swaddled in new, fine-spun wool, a gift from the farmer's wife, and sucked on a teat of goat's milk and honey, fashioned out of linen by Biton.

"Or you could, if you chose, master," suggested Biton thoughtfully, "name her after an ox – or, perhaps even a bison."

Orpheus chuckled. "No little girl would be pleased with such a name, I think, dear Biton."

The poet was of good cheer, now that he was on a well-cleared path again, the day becoming warm with the brilliant sunlight.

But he was troubled, at the same time, by what he saw around him. While some farms were rich, populated by plump ducks and fat hens, many farmsteads were bleak, and several of the field folk they passed were hollow-eyed, stooping to free their wooden pitchforks from the thick and clinging mud.

Orpheus wondered if the impoverished men and women he passed might be relations of the infant Melia, brokenhearted at having to surrender the infant to her fate – but thankful, too, that the gods had found a capable-looking guardian.

"Are we to travel the world with this mild-hearted Melia?" Biton was inquiring. The prince's assistant was a welcoming youth, of ample cheer, but he was sometimes jealous of his master's attentions.

Orpheus gave a laugh. He was about to reassure the lad

that soon they would no doubt find a loving home for the infant girl.

But a sweet sound stopped him in his tracks.

Biton crept ahead, peering down the path.

The music of a stream rose upward through the grove, accompanied by the sound of women singing.

"Master, I hear a most pleasant chorus," Biton said at last.

"I hear them, too," Orpheus answered, rocking the drowsing infant in his arms. "Go on, Biton, and see who they might be."

"They could be wood nymphs," responded Biton. "Naked and dancing, and they might blind the eyes in my head for looking."

Such things did happen, it was said – dryads and goddesses were careful defenders of their modesty.

But there could be no doubt. Female voices somewhere not far off sang the hymn of Juno, praising the wisdom of women over the many follies of their husbands. Surely, thought Orpheus, they were mortal women, not wood spirits. And they had astonishingly lovely voices – one of them in particular.

"But if you insist, master," Biton was saying, "I shall investigate."

"Women – mortal human ladies! They are bathing in a stream," said Biton excitedly on his return. "Handsome women, too, Prince

Orpheus — if I may say so. And one of them has the most beautiful voice of all."

But the singing had stopped.

Footsteps whispered through the undergrowth, and a man with a lance stood before the two travelers, leveling his weapon at Biton's master.

FOUR

THE YOUNG STRANGER wore a brightly polished bronze chest plate, and well-cured leather. The broad point of his spear was bright, and the pommel of the sword at his hip was the finest gold.

Orpheus spoke the proper greeting, introducing himself formally – including the names of his illustrious parents, and his recent ports of call, Lesbos and the sea kingdoms of the Bosporus.

It was important for a wayfarer to share such information –

out of courtesy, and to help prove that a traveler was neither a fugitive from some lawful power, nor a ghost. Escapees from the underworld were thought to be angry and vindictive, and not given to civil conversation.

"I am called Lachesis, Prince Orpheus," responded the young stranger, lowering his lance just slightly. "My father rules this kingdom, and I do what I can to shelter my sister."

Orpheus bowed politely, and watched to be sure that Biton gave an even deeper show of respect. "I've heard of you, gracious prince," said the poet. "You are the worthy brother of the famous Eurydice."

"Noble poet," responded the prince, "although your name is praised from shore to mountain summit, I must ask you bluntly: Is it your habit for you and your servant to watch innocent women as they bathe?"

"Oh, and is it right for a brother to hide in the reeds," retorted Biton, "and do the very same thing?"

The infant in Orpheus's arms stirred sleepily.

Perhaps the sight of the baby softened the royal brother's suspicion. Or perhaps it was Orpheus's good-natured answer. "The gods love a warmhearted welcome, Prince Lachesis — and a traveler who deserves one."

Lachesis called out, and three or four other armed figures appeared along the path, their weapons glinting among the willows.

"Brother, what intruders are these?" inquired a woman's voice.

"She's the one, master," whispered Biton excitedly, "who sang more beautifully than all the others."

Mortals were thought to be dependent on divine beings for nearly every passion or skill. Battle courage was endowed by Mars, sound judgment by Minerva, and a reciter of lengthy epics was grateful to Mnemosyne, the goddess of memory. Even love was believed to be empowered by a deity – and a playful, potent one at that.

Some said that Eros was a boylike god, armed with a quiver of barbs. Others held that the god of sudden love more closely resembled a well-sinewed youth, lancing the human heart with a spear. Orpheus knew many lyrics about the god's caprice. However, until that moment the son of Calliope had believed such tales were merely pretty verses. Surely, he had always thought, a sensible traveler like himself could not be struck dumb with unexpected passion.

But at that moment Prince Orpheus could not make a sound.

"Do you not understand our speech, good traveler?" inquired Princess Eurydice with an air of friendly inquisitiveness.

"We heard the sound of beautiful singing, Princess," Orpheus managed to respond. "And we quite naturally had to stop and listen."

The princess wore a soft-woven chiton, a flowing garment, with embroidered seams of gold-bright thread. Her hair was dark, and her eyes were dark, too, like the night seas off Numidia.

"And is this the renowned poet," the young woman was asking her brother, "whose music is a legend among gods and men?"

As she made this query, an attendant placed a blue cloak around her shoulders, and helped the princess fasten it at her throat with an ivory brooch.

"No doubt my powers have been exaggerated," offered Orpheus, with courteous modesty.

"I have learned not to believe very much of what I'm told," said Eurydice. "By any man."

Orpheus offered a silent prayer to Venus, who had power over both the human heart and the playful, often spiteful Eros.

Help me, soul-stirring goddess, the poet prayed.

To win this woman's love.

FIVE

EURYDICE HAD DREAMED of meeting the famous singer and poet long before this moment.

She saw that Orpheus was well favored, and the musical instrument he carried gave off a lovely glow. And he had a thoughtful eye, and a gentle voice as he spoke, the soft tones of his speech giving little hint of the fabled power of his song.

But the princess had encountered a string of charming men – noble travelers who had sought to court her. Hippeus of Cos had been a powerfully built man, with a kindhearted laugh. He had impressed her deeply at first – but one morning she spied him beating a servant for bringing him day-old bread for breakfast, and she banished Hippeus from the kingdom.

Likewise, Zelus from far-off Sicily had pleased her with his charming looks and many amusing stories. But when her brother Lachesis ordered him not to kick the household dogs, Zelus had called his prospective brother-in-law a weakhearted ninny. That had been the sudden end of that courtship, too.

Eurydice's heart quickened as Orpheus drew nearer to her, and her spirit was further lightened by the sight of his tenderness toward the unexplained infant in his arms. But she had learned to mistrust men, and her feelings about them. She was, she feared, too easily won over.

Besides, no doubt this legendary young man had been married at some point in his journeys, and she had not heard the tidings. What other explanation could there be for the baby in his sheltering arms?

She breathed an inward prayer to Juno that a married man – even the world-renowned poet – might not steal her heart.

For his part, Orpheus could barely meet her gaze.

"What do we see here?" queried the princess with a skeptical smile. "Is the famous Orpheus a married father, carrying his infant through the woodland?"

"My master rescued this baby girl from a pack of ravenous hounds, my lady," asserted Biton. "As the gods allowed it," he added, unwilling to give offense to any divine power that might be listening.

Eurydice's features softened, as her brother's had, as she took a long moment to peer curiously at the infant in Orpheus's arms. Certainly her tone changed as she asked, "And so you do not have a wife, good Orpheus, weaving you a new travel cloak back home?"

"My lady," said Orpheus, "poetry is my only home, and the truth is that I have no wife."

"Have you ever heard such talk!" said Eurydice to the ladies around her, and there was kindhearted – but very definite – laughter. "'Poetry is my only home,'" mocked the princess gently.

Eurydice put a hand on the baby's cheek, and the infant stirred. The princess turned to one of her ladies. "Carry this baby into the shade of the trees," she directed one of her serving women. "I think the sunlight troubles her."

Orpheus was reluctant to part with Melia.

"Dear poet, you must think us heartless folk," said the princess, her manner all the more welcoming now. "We shall find a caring home and hearth for this lovely Melia," she continued with a smile, "in honor of the poet who saved her life."

With a quiet prayer of thanks to the gods, Orpheus surrendered the swaddled baby to the attendants.

Orpheus approached the palace outbuildings beside this remarkable princess, and at times he could make no more conversation than a mule.

"Many men travel far to offer me golden flattery, Prince Orpheus," said Eurydice at last.

"I am sometimes capable of spirited speech, Princess Eurydice," he replied. "But for the moment Venus favors me with an honest silence. I hope I do not seem discourteous."

Eurydice, too, had heard tell of unpredictable Eros. Some said he struck the heart with a javelin, while others said he used a relentless whip. Could such stories be more than empty legend? Before this moment men had both attracted her and deceived her, but this lightning in her pulse was something she had not sensed before.

"I'm certain I cut a rude figure," the poet was saying, "mud-splashed as I am."

"Your appearance, dear poet," the princess allowed, "does not displease me, it is fair to say."

"I am grateful to hear it," said Orpheus.

"The truth is, Prince Orpheus," continued Eurydice, with an

air of careful modesty, "I look forward to learning of your many travels – and perhaps you will go so far as to share your poetry with me."

Orpheus took heart at this, but before he could offer his enthusiastic assent, one of the guards uttered a cry of warning.

"Stay back," he cautioned everyone within earshot. "It's yet another serpent."

After quick work with his lance, the long, lithe creature twisted on the paving stones.

"Some people say that these are omens of some future ill," said the princess. "A lynx stole over the palace wall and killed nine sacred doves just last week, and a bull went mad in the marketplace, crippling a carter."

A guard held up the still twitching body of a venomous asp, a slowly writhing, hooded reptile.

"Good-hearted poet," said Eurydice, concern in her voice, "I am afraid that my father's kingdom may prove dangerous to you."

2

ſIX

KING LYCOMEDE, Eurydice's father, lifted his wine cup and laughed contentedly.

"Be kind enough to sing for us, Prince Orpheus," said the king. "Nothing would please me more."

He was a round-faced, silver-haired man, with a merry eye. One of the king's first acts in the poet's presence was to ordain a safe and prosperous home for the infant Melia – a promising adoption with loving parents, the respected potter Alxion and his wife Alope. Orpheus was grateful to the monarch.

Music was welcome after conversation, and Orpheus was happy to oblige with the most heart-stirring songs. The royal court had dined well, on roast pig and smoked tuna – and yet, in the poet's heart, someone's absence was deeply felt. Men and women in Lycomede's kingdom dined separately, as was proper throughout the Greek world. But never before had the poet so missed the companionship of a certain woman.

Soon, thought Orpheus – I must see her again soon.

When the poet finished a song about the safe harbor of Chios, and how the keels of every ship dreamed of entering the restful waters of that isle, Orpheus sipped his wine. This court drank their wine *akretos* – undiluted with water. This was not usual among Greeks, who valued moderation, and Orpheus felt that his senses were already addled enough by his passion for the princess.

"I wonder," the king was asking now, "if you could teach my son to sing that poem you recited earlier – about Diana at her bath."

"I'll be pleased and honored to," said Orpheus with a smile. "If Lachesis so desires it – and as the gods permit."

The king shook his head with a bitter smile. "Talk of pleasing the gods, dear poet, does not move my heart. When my beautiful wife, Halia, died of a fever just after childbirth, I turned away from any belief in the immortals."

"Good king," said Orpheus, "I am sorry to learn of your grief."

"My daughter never knew her mother's kiss," said the king with a sigh, "and I came to believe that no god existed who would allow such sorrow."

"I was hoping that our noble guest could tell us more about divine Diana," said Lachesis, respectful toward his father, but hoping, too, for some further word about the immortals.

"I am sorry to say," responded Orpheus, "that I have never set eyes on that undying goddess."

"Of course you haven't seen her, Orpheus," said the king with a sad laugh. "Those tales are merely fireside tittle-tattle."

"They say the divine Phoebus Apollo," retorted the prince, "gave Prince Orpheus his well-crafted silver lyre."

"This pretty instrument here," chortled the king incredulously, "the one leaning against the footstool of our guest?"

"So they say," asserted his son.

"We don't seriously believe that," laughed the king, "do we?"

"You will think me an ungrateful guest," said Orpheus, rising.

"Tell us, please, noble Orpheus," pleaded Eurydice's brother, "if you have seen the god of daylight."

Poets of many lands still chanted of the day, many years before, when Apollo had allowed his beloved mortal son Phaeton to take the reins of sunlight's chariot. Their verses still commemorated falcons falling in flames, and rivers flash-scalded into steam.

Apollo had become a more thoughtful god, it was told, ever afterward, and had tried to make amends to mortals by helping poets create stories – and in particular by giving Prince Orpheus a lyre of perfect pitch and dazzling beauty.

Orpheus could see it all again that instant in his heart – the day he received the lyre from the divinity's own hands. The god's voice had been music, and his laugh sweeter than the west wind.

"On a cold day, Lachesis," said Orpheus at last, breaking off his reverie, "my lyre is still warm from Apollo's touch."

SEVEN

IT WAS NOT until the following night that Orpheus walked with Eurydice beside the royal pond.

That day Biton had asked, eagerly, "What poem will you use to win her heart, master?"

The poet had sighed — if only he could think of one.

Orpheus would not have admitted as much to anyone, but there was, in all his travels, more than a little loneliness. True, Biton was a steady companion, but Orpheus found the men and women he met too easily dazzled by his reputation, and sometimes too easily charmed by the simplest song.

Bright-haired Calliope had been an absent mother, always gone to some distant corner of the sea to inspire yet another talented poet. And the prince's royal father had resigned himself to an absent, immortal spouse by planting groves, building bridges, and seeing that his kingdom was at peace. Orpheus had set forth on his ceaseless travels because there was no place for him in a home that was empty except for the busy footsteps of servants.

Although he was still a young man, Orpheus had seen much of the world. Now, walking beside the princess, Orpheus felt that he wanted to be nowhere but right where he was.

The fishpond was dark in the starlight, and a sleepy carp rose to the surface, nibbling Orpheus's fingers and darting back into the depths.

From far off, the sound of song drifted from the servants' quarters. Biton's voice could be heard calling out the tune, the ever-popular ditty "Goat and Flute." Orpheus had been working to teach Biton the complexities of music, and while the young servant still had much to learn, the sound brought a smile to Orpheus's lips.

A spearman stood in the distance, keeping watch against the possibility of danger. A rush of laughter reached them from another quarter, along with the distant rattling of dice. The king was at play, and — judging by the sound — he was winning.

"Perhaps you begin to believe me," said Eurydice, after a silence, "when I assure you that I will be unmoved by your powers." In truth, she knew, it was all she could do to keep from blurting out her love.

"You did agree to come out from the women's quarters," said Orpheus happily. "And agree to walk with me down to this royal pond." He was pleased to find a woman who was not easily captured by his reputation — and he sensed a warm affection in her voice.

"Do not read much into that, dear Orpheus," she responded. "Or into the fact that I do admire a man who is kindhearted." Caution restrained her — a lingering fear that, despite all the evidence, the poet might prove another, all the more galling, disappointment.

"I can only hope," responded the poet, "that the gods will answer my prayers."

"I believe you are a good-natured man, Orpheus," said Eurydice, "a loving master and a poet blessed by the immortals. But I am afraid that perhaps you rely too much on the gods for your easy triumphs."

Before he could answer, Eurydice put out her hand and raised a finger to her lips.

Ahead of them in the poor light, a young swan was fluttering.

Its companions were dim shapes far across the pond, but this lone straggler kicked and struggled, unable to join them.

As Eurydice approached the struggling fowl, Orpheus cautioned her, "Be careful – swans are not as sweet-natured as they appear."

The princess knelt and stroked the white cygnet. The proud waterfowl grumbled and snapped at first, but grew gradually calm as she cradled one webbed foot in her hand.

"The servants catch fish for our meals," explained Eurydice. "Sometimes the nets tear, and float where no one can see them. This princely bird has been caught in a bit of such webbing."

Her fingers worked quickly.

Soon the swan waddled free, grunted solemnly at the two of them, and set forth across the water.

Continuing through the torch-lit half-dark, Orpheus and Eurydice wandered out to the venerable temple of Minerva. The poet was glad they were visiting this sacred place. Surely, he thought, I need divine guidance in wooing such a woman.

But the poet stopped as the two approached the holy site, and gave a cry of dismay.

"Eurydice, please tell me," gasped Orpheus, "what terrible thing has happened here?"

EIGHT

MARBLE COLUMNS had tumbled and grown thick with moss.

Ivy had cloaked the steps, dark leaves glowing dimly in the starlight. The inner chamber, where the goddess could be made welcome should she ever visit this kingdom, was bare and open to the sky, the temple floors dense with weeds.

"My father says," explained the princess, "that we should not be prayerful, like the men and women in other lands." She added, "The small temple of Juno where I pray is kept quite pretty."

"But the queen of wisdom must be sorrowful," said Orpheus, "when she sees this crumbling marble step."

By night the vista from the ruined temple was only an abyss of empty darkness, the hills and far-off ocean sullen and invisible under the stars. Something about the sight gave the poet a shiver. Orpheus loved daylight, with its lively animals and laughter – he knew that darkness was no human being's friend.

The poet reached down to tug at a weed. "I am afraid for your father's kingdom, dear Eurydice."

Some said that only the sweetest herbs grew in a temple, even one lost to ruin like this. Orpheus placed the leaves gently on the broken marble altar.

The poet gave voice to a poem he crafted at that moment.

> *Forgive the rain,*
> *Eurydice, the rain and the wind,*
> *for not loving you as I do.*

A presence approached from the darkness above, a pale shadow slipping across the stars, called forth by Orpheus's voice.

Silver-feathered plumage circled closer, the breeze from the beating wings stirring Orpheus's hair as he reached up into the darkness.

The poet took a great owl onto his outstretched hand.

Some said that Minerva occasionally took the form of a feathered hunter like this. The warm talons gripped the poet's wrist, and the black, all-seeing eyes looked into his own.

The princess was unable to make a sound, shocked into wonder.

The owl turned her night-conquering eyes toward Eurydice. And then the luminous bird spread her wings and glided off, lofting upward through the starlight.

"Orpheus, do you think this is how you can win me?" asked Eurydice breathlessly. "By showing off your wonderful powers?"

Orpheus made an attempt to respond, but Eurydice silenced him with a kiss.

Did Orpheus ask Eurydice to be his wife by whispering a poem, or did he employ ordinary speech, like any mortal?

No one will ever know.

Later that night Eurydice knelt in the small temple of Juno, the tidy marble interior and starlit columns a contrast to the forgotten sanctuary of Minerva.

She thanked the divine consort of Jupiter for bringing the poet to her father's kingdom.

She did not forget to add a prayer for her future husband's health.

"Please, immortal Juno," she breathed, "may he encounter no harm."

NINE

KING LYCOMEDE clapped his hands and danced when he received the news.

"My permission?" he chortled. "My dear Orpheus, do you think me a madman? I prayed for this, even in my godless heart!"

The king called for the minister of ceremonies, an official who arrived dabbing at his lips with a linen napkin.

"I decree it!" cried the king with a laugh. "No sad faces will be allowed anywhere in my kingdom."

"My lord king, as you wish!" said the minister, looking with dazed amazement from his monarch to Orpheus.

"We'll have a glorious wedding," cried the king, "and every single mortal under the sky is invited."

Plans for the wedding began, and they took a fortnight to unfold, even with eager hands helping every hour.

Some of the preparations were traditional throughout Greek lands, such as the torchlight procession being readied so that the celebrants could sing the solemn, beautiful hymns of Hymen, the mysterious deity who oversaw weddings.

Other details, like the great bronze bathtub being smithed for Eurydice's ritual pre-wedding bath, were peculiar to her kingdom. New drinking cups of silver were hammered into shape in the artisans' shops, and garlands of agate and gold leaf were spun, rare diadems for the wedding march.

Rich delicacies were planned for the banquets, rare fish ordered from the seaside villages, and a command went out for pigs' wombs, to be simmered and basted to perfection – a dish prized by folk of that land. Flute girls gathered from far-flung farmlands, and oboe players gathered, too, bright-eyed in anticipation at playing music in the presence of Prince Orpheus.

*　　*　　*

"I have decided that I do not need new clothes," Biton said one afternoon a few days later, when he and his master had a moment together.

A tailor had just left the two of them, bowing his way out, taking measurements for a new purple mantle to be worn by Prince Orpheus. Such dyes were rare and expensive, produced from the flesh of scarce shellfish.

"I've ordered you fine garments," protested Orpheus, "and a new mantle, with that pear-blossom pattern you admired in Rodos all along the hem."

"I'll make it a point of pride," insisted Biton, "to wear my worn traveling cloak, and my hat, too, singing Hymen's hymn, walking along looking simple and plain."

"You will have your hair dressed with oil of nard," said Orpheus, referring to a precious, sweet-smelling perfume, "and in that embroidered mantle no one will have eyes for the groom, let alone the bride."

"That's all to the good," said Biton. "Because then perhaps I'll attract the attention of a new master."

"My dear Biton, whatever are you thinking?"

"Well, surely you won't be needing the attentions of a servant named Biton once you are married."

"Biton, I give you my word," said the poet with a smile. "You and I are spun together, like two strands of rope."

The young servant stirred, and scurried off to the well to see the pretty women of the palace, perhaps, and to fetch his master a fresh pitcher of water.

He kept his happy eyes downcast. It was not wise, Biton knew, to let the Fates see a mortal so full of hope.

TEN

ONE MORNING, not long before the wedding, Orpheus paid a visit to the home of Alxion the potter and his wife Alope, the adopted parents of the baby Melia.

To his surprise, Eurydice had arrived beforehand, and knelt singing a soothing lyric beside the sleeping infant.

"Why are you surprised to see me here?" asked the princess with a smile, when her song was done. "After all, Orpheus, I have good reason to be grateful to little Melia – you were holding her in your arms when I first set eyes on you."

The baby was drowsing peacefully in a blanket of soft-combed lamb's wool. Alxion was eager to show the prince the snug and neatly crafted cradle he had built of poplar wood so that, as the earnest potter put it, "Not even the north wind will shake her sleep."

Alope modestly showed the poet the mantle she was weaving of blue- and gold-dyed yarn, so when the child was old enough to accompany her mother to the water well, no winter mist could chill her.

It gave Orpheus great happiness to see the joy in their eyes.

And he was touched, too, at Eurydice's generous nature. The princess did not depart without leaving a wreath of silver laurel leaves with the parents, affixed to the head of the cradle.

Before she left, Eurydice brushed the infant's forehead with her lips, and Melia stirred happily.

As the wedding day grew near, as custom decreed, the couple were rarely allowed to set eyes on each other.

It was not considered good luck to let betrothed lovers spend much time together now, and laughing but insistent women gently pushed Orpheus away from Eurydice's gate when he arrived with his lyre.

He did linger outside the high-walled refuge, where he could hear her singing her favorites, poems in praise of Juno. And he did see her plainly, once – on a sunny afternoon, as she made her way down to the well.

Orpheus had been waiting there, and while servants and matrons laughingly suggested he fly off like a jackdaw and leave honest women alone, it was a tradition that men and women – even when they were betrothed – could meet at the watering place to make conversation.

"Tonight!" breathed Orpheus when he was close to her. *We'll meet tonight.*

"I've a new poem for you," whispered Orpheus when passion allowed him to speak that evening.

The white walls of the royal dwellings reflected the soft light of stars. A gentle breeze blew, swirling Eurydice's mantle, and the round opening of the wellhead gave off a hush.

And yet there was no telling what divine powers might be listening – the gods were said to be fascinated with humans and their loves and woes. Rumor herself was thought to be a persistent being, in form somewhat like a young woman. She was an assistant to Mercury, messenger of the gods, and was said to have ears that could hear a promise broken far at sea.

Orpheus had nothing to fear from any divine power, but he wanted his song to be for Eurydice's ears only. And so he began to sing softly, words that he had woven and reworked all the hours they had spent apart.

"Who's there?" cried a distant voice, interrupting the first verse.

An armored figure tramped forth out of the lamplight.

"Oh, my lord prince and my lady princess, do forgive me, please," said the helmeted guard, starlight reflecting from the point of his spear. "We have an extra watch out tonight," the guardsman continued. "They say that a griffin attacked a mule driver out by the olive grove this afternoon."

"Was the poor man hurt?" asked Eurydice.

"Oh, my lady princess," laughed the guard, "our muleteers are made of heartwood."

But the guard waited, and would not depart, adding at last, "If you'll forgive me, the king's orders are that it is not safe to be out tonight."

"I'll hear the rest of your poem, Orpheus," whispered Eurydice to her husband-to-be, "tomorrow – on our wedding night."

Juno, look
to the apple blossom,
protect it,
cupping your hand against the frost.

Orpheus was disappointed at the delay.

But he looked forward all the more ardently to singing these living words to Eurydice – his new wife.

ELEVEN

THE WEDDING CEREMONY was as grand as the exultant king had wished.

The procession was splendid, every voice joining in the hymn to Hymen. Torchlights carried by the throng illuminated the early evening. The princess stopped at the newly garlanded temple of Juno, and she left a lock of her hair on the altar, as tradition dictated.

Then she continued on to her father's main hall, where further hymns to Hymen were chorused, accompanied by flutes and tambours – vibrant, soul-stirring music.

But as Orpheus took the hand of Eurydice, in harmony with ancient ceremony, some small event troubled him.

One of the torches in the great hallway flickered and expired, giving off a plume of white smoke.

Perhaps Orpheus was the only celebrant who observed this. Even as he completed singing his wedding hymn, he added an additional, silent prayer – to Apollo, the lord of daylight.

Protect this marriage, he earnestly prayed.

And may that spume of pale, twisting smoke not prove to be an omen.

The celebrations went on through the night, but at one point not long before morning, as was proper, Orpheus excused himself.

Following wedding custom, the bridegroom would wait in his chambers while a further procession, of the bride and her friends, took her through her old neighborhood, dancing to the sound of tambours, clapping hands, and much laughter. Then, after the gathered friends sang a wedding song, all would retire, leaving the newly married couple to the delights of the approaching dawn.

Biton was nowhere to be seen, but he had prepared the wedding bed, and left lamps alight and a pitcher of pink wine.

It was usual for the groom to feel some impatience as he

awaited the approach of his bride. But now the poet paced his room, aware that birds were stirring. Dawn was upon them, and yet he was still alone.

Surely, he thought, this time-honored procession was taking too long. And the palace and the surrounding neighborhood – hadn't they seemed to have fallen too silent?

At that moment a cry startled Orpheus.

Somewhere far off – a wail of anguish.

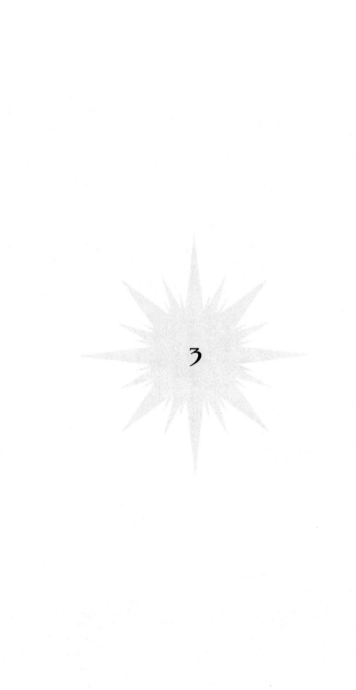

3

TWELVE

ALARMED, ORPHEUS JOINED the stream of men and women hurrying from the palace buildings toward the royal pond.

Lachesis, tears on his cheeks, turned from where he crouched beside the fishpond. His gold-hilted sword was in his hand.

A viper writhed and struggled, cut into several pieces, at the royal brother's feet. The snake's head snapped at the early sunlight, fangs flashing, and its tail lashed the spreading puddle of blood.

"Orpheus," tearstained Lachesis managed to say, "we are too late."

The words meant little to Orpheus at first, stunned and confused as he was.

Questions awakened and vanished in his mind before the poet could find the power to put them into words. Women were weeping, garlanded in their wedding finery, and a guard began to bawl, hammering the ground with the butt of his spear.

Pale and unmoving, Eurydice lay sprawling among the tall grasses.

"She was about to conclude the wedding procession, Prince Orpheus," Lachesis explained, with a broken voice. "She was leading the singing, impatient to reach you."

Two bleeding holes in her ankle showed where the viper had buried its fangs.

Orpheus knelt beside her, too shocked to trust his senses.

He spoke her name.

He called to her again, but still she did not respond.

The son of Calliope, grandson of Jupiter, knew well that his beloved was already gone, but he summoned all of his powers as he put his hands on her, feeling for a pulse and at the same time murmuring a prayer.

Then the grieving poet gathered her into his arms and sang, a full-voiced, sorrow-broken cry, calling to the immortals to return Eurydice to life.

THIRTEEN

NOT A SINGLE SMITH worked metal throughout the far-
flung towns and villages, and in the fields no plowman
parted soil.

Lamplight in every dwelling was smoky and thin, the wicks
left untrimmed, and no one spoke above a whisper.

The kingdom mourned.

No one, however, grieved more deeply than Orpheus.

He did not speak, except to comfort the king, who sat in the broad oak chair, his royal throne. The bereaved father did not respond to any human voice except that of the poet. And the only sign he gave of hearing Orpheus's condolences was to reach out and take the poet's hand each time he entered the room.

The muse's son did not touch his lyre. He did not even want to set eyes on the silver instrument, and draped it with a cloth. He did not sing a syllable, day after day, and even the prettiest of birdsong in the eaves gave him no pleasure.

Orpheus fasted – as was proper – while the funeral pyre, cords of laurel wood, was prepared in the main courtyard. A palace that had been flush with flowers and wine was now colorless and silent, ashes scattered over the courtyards. Grief singers – women well rehearsed at dirges – keened hourly beside the lifeless body of Eurydice.

The princess was cremated. Her ashes were secured in an urn, and buried in a place sacred to her family, not far from the temple of Juno.

After the rites were completed, Orpheus did not take in more than a swallow or two of watered wine. He touched no food.

"Please try a bite of this bread, master," said Biton one evening as Orpheus fastened his mantle, preparing to pay his respects once more to the king.

Orpheus turned back from the doorway, saying nothing.

"Rich-crusted bread, good master," said Biton encouragingly, holding up a plate. "The bakers have fired up their ovens for the first time in many days."

Orpheus lifted a gentle hand, declining the nourishment.

"I shall grow feeble," said Biton, as though to himself. "I shall waste to a bundle of sticks out of worry for my royal prince."

Lachesis paced slowly before the king's chamber.

He embraced the poet lovingly when he arrived and said, "I am worried, dear Orpheus. The king is far weaker today. He will not open his eyes or give any sign of hearing what I say."

A bearded man in a long blue tunic, the garb of learned men in this kingdom, approached the two of them.

"Doctor, how is your patient?" asked Orpheus.

The physician hesitated.

"Be truthful with us," urged the poet.

"The king cannot live for long as he is, good gentlemen," said the physician. "I am being truthful when I say that unless he stirs himself and begins to eat and drink, before long he will join his daughter in the underworld."

FOURTEEN

BITON LEAPED UP when Orpheus returned to his chamber.

Something had changed in his master's stride, some new determination, that gave the servant hope.

The poet approached the lyre of Apollo, hidden under a length of fine wool. He did not remove the cloth at once, but took a long moment to prepare himself for the sight of the silver frame – sometimes, in the midst of sorrow, it is hard to look upon a thing of beauty.

He ran his hands over the warmth of the lyre, and when he touched a string with a fingertip, the single note – insistent but so nearly silent – quickened his heart.

"We have to help our friends, Biton," explained Orpheus to his companion's questioning glance, "when their sorrow is so great."

Orpheus played for King Lycomede and Prince Lachesis.

The music was soul-quieting, notes that hung in the silence long after he had plucked them.

But still the poet did not sing.

He did not lift his voice – no power could move him to poetry.

And for a long hour that afternoon no song was needed. The chords Orpheus plucked were enough to cause the king to turn, and look out for the first time in days, gazing toward the honey-colored light of late day. The king watched the gray doves in the courtyard fluttering upward, uttering their low courting songs.

The king spoke at last.

After a week of silence, his voice was little more than a whisper.

"Orpheus," said the king, with an effort to make himself understood, "please sing of Persephone and Pluto in the world of night."

Orpheus was slightly surprised that the grieving, skeptical king might seek solace in a somber – and religious – poem.

The poet obliged, however, with the hymn about the lord of the underworld and his stolen bride, who became the queen of that lightless place. Orpheus was pleased to see that the song caused the bereaved father to nod slowly in rhythm, and the sight of the king's lips moving silently to the time-honored verses touched the poet deeply.

Orpheus ceased to play, and stilled the vibrant strings with the flat of his hand. The song echoed, as did the last music from the lyre, and the young man waited for silence to gather before he stood and exclaimed, "Now I know what I must do!"

"Play another song, dear boy," said the king. "That is all I require of your sweet nature."

"I shall journey," said Orpheus, "to that unknown place."

"Where?" asked the king, in the first stirrings of alarm. But when King Lycomede saw the resolve in the poet's eyes, he burst out, "Surely you won't risk traveling there, my dear Orpheus!"

The land of the dead was shunned, as the king well knew — no living traveler went there by choice, or even considered doing such a thing.

"I shall go into the kingdom of the dead," said Orpheus simply, "and, with the permission of the gods, I will bring Eurydice home with me."

"Orpheus, you may find yourself able to travel into the lightless kingdom," said the king, his voice ragged with dread. "But I fear that even the son of a muse will be unable to journey home again."

FIFTEEN

MASTER AND SERVANT stood beside the sea, seeking the sea captain's help. The salt breeze stirred their hair, and the sunlight danced on the wide, blue water.

Orpheus looked on patiently as Biton asserted, "If my master wishes to sing for the queen of darkness and her lord, who am I to question him?"

"Forgive me," said the red-haired captain, "but I cannot accept this great honor."

"Please, captain – this day is the single most fortunate of your life," said Biton, using his best and most persuasive manners. Biton's voice was hoarse with the dread he felt contemplating their destination. But he would not have it said that Biton was an incapable servant, unable to bargain for a dish of figs – or a ship's berth – as duty required.

"Net menders all over the world will forever assert that Idas, son of Aphareus," continued the captain, laying a broad, freckled hand on his own chest, "took the famous poet to his life's end."

"My master," continued Biton, as though he had not been interrupted, "has a purse of fresh-minted gold to make the voyage all the sweeter for you."

"I will not let it be said," said Idas, with a stubborn but fading intensity, "that the fair ship *Actis* took the son of a divine muse to – that dark place I will not name."

Orpheus looked on, an appreciative smile on his lips as Biton took a step closer to the captain. "Look at the ropes, Captain Idas," said Biton, "how tattered they are; the sail, how weather-stained. Now you can make this ship look proud again, as I am sure she once was." Biton thrust a heavy purse into the captain's hands. "And win a name in one of my master's songs."

The captain stirred at the sound of this.

"Think of how round and satisfying the verses will be," added Biton, "when my master sings of Captain Idas and his brave ship."

The captain sighed – and at last gave a bow.

"And my men," called Captain Idas, his crew stirring to watch the famous poet step on board the ship, each seaman too awe-struck to make a sound. "You'll sing of my crew – how able they were and eager to lend a hand."

Orpheus gave a sad but willing smile.

"And with the help of divine Mercury, worthy prince," added the captain, "we'll see about changing your mind about your destination."

At this Biton could only murmur to himself, or to whatever divine power might overhear, "May it be so!"

SIXTEEN

THE ROWERS PLIED their oars, their labor made lighter by Orpheus, strumming on his lyre.

"Tarry with us, noble poet!" a mariner begged, as he rested on his oar, the wind bellying the stained, oft-mended sail. "Prince Orpheus, don't go down into that unnamed place."

Among sailors it was considered bad luck to refer to the realm of the dead. Indeed, people rarely spoke of the underworld at all, but folk had a general idea what sort of kingdom it was. The spirits of the dead were known as shades, and the most fortunate of those slept in honorable peace in that domain. Unhappy shades, however, were said to wander certain regions of that unknown landscape, harried by winged Furies – the tireless spirits of revenge.

Orpheus knew how to be a welcome shipmate. He gave a smile – tinged with his deep sadness – and began to pluck chords again, leaning back against the mast.

He sang of the ship *Actis*, whose name meant "beam of light." No ship was as sturdy-beamed as that spirited vessel, he sang, and no ship's wake was as silver-bright under the stars.

Wet from their brief wade through the surf toward land, Biton and Orpheus waved at their seafaring companions as the ship turned about.

The vessel worked her way from the black rocks of the shore, oars stirring the sea. Cries of farewell reached them through the fresh morning wind, and Biton secretly prayed once more that his noble master might change his mind.

"Sail away with us, Prince Orpheus," called the red-haired captain, but the poet gave a decisive gesture of farewell.

Soon the ship had cocked her sail into the wind and swept away from the broad coast – even the hardiest mariners wanted to avoid the legendary entryway into the dark world.

Orpheus wasted little time, taking long strides away from the sea, and expecting Biton to keep the pace.

As the two travelers approached the rocky slope, birdsong faded and grew silent. The wind died, too, as they made their way toward a tall grove of black trees, like a forest carbonized by flash fire and left standing.

Soon the legendary grove of black poplars, the outer limits to the entryway into Hades' domain, stood tall around them.

"If we see a ghost, master," quavered Biton, "how should we greet it?"

SEVENTEEN

"WE WILL BE as polite to the dead," suggested the poet, "as we try to be to the living."

"I was hoping we still had many hours," said Biton, "or even a few more days to journey on some friendly, sunny road."

Orpheus laughed thoughtfully. "I would not mind a few more minutes of sunlight myself, Biton," he admitted. "But every moment I spend breathing morning air is another without Eurydice."

The leaves hung shiny and motionless in the sunlight,

stems that never, year after year, released from their ebony branches. This was not a recently scorched grove, torched by a fiery calamity, but a woodland turned to eternal stone. With the passage of the two travelers, branches stirred and the trees gave off a glassy music.

The gates could not be said to be barriers at all – they were stone slabs on iron hinges left ajar by some unknown power long ago. There was no need to warn any seeker to shrink back from the dark chasm, the entrance into the stone. No bird called, even from the distant world of morning.

Orpheus made his way into the gateway, with every show of confidence, as though resolve required a degree of speed. But the poet shrank back as the first deep shadow of the entryway fell over him.

He retreated a few strides, back into the muted twilight of the grove.

Orpheus spoke thoughtfully, like a man realizing for the first time the scope of his pilgrimage. "There's no need for you to follow, dear Biton."

"Master, I am yours," said Biton, his voice shaking, "to command."

"Here, Biton, take most of the gold from my purse. Nearby villages will honor a traveler from the wide world, and you deserve a feast."

"Master, can it be that you yourself do not want to set eyes on Persephone and her lord?"

Orpheus did not address the question directly. "I cannot ask anyone else," answered the poet, "to brave that dark place."

"So let us both go to a village where the lambs are plump, and the coals hot," suggested Biton, "and dine on honeycomb."

"I will see Eurydice again," said Orpheus simply.

Biton smiled ruefully. He understood well that Eurydice had been a rare woman. Nevertheless Biton was not ashamed to point out – silently, to himself – that sorrow had its dignity, and that mourning was both proper and necessary. No other human traveled into the underworld after a lost bride.

"I do not have faith in my courage, good Biton," continued Orpheus. "I don't even have faith in the strength of my love. Loving men have mourned before, and the world of darkness showed no effort to repay their loss."

"Other men and women weep, master," assented Biton at once, "but in the end they live to enjoy good, long lives."

"Poetry," Orpheus said, "will win Eurydice back from the darkness."

Without a further word the poet stepped again through the shadow entrance.

And Biton followed, into the world of night.

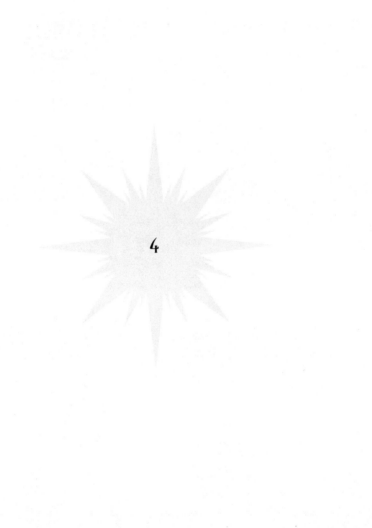

4

EIGHTEEN

BITON TRAILED the poet, the two stepping cautiously down the slippery path, lichen-scabbed rocks on either side.

Lingering daylight dissolved quickly to an absence of any light at all. And yet that perfect darkness was diminished gradually by an otherworldly illumination, given off by mineral veins of persistent luminescence and dimly glowing stones.

"Biton, be careful!" cautioned Orpheus, pointing out a gushing stream across their path.

Orpheus led the way, reaching back to take Biton's hand, pulling him across the shocking-cold stream. But Biton's foot slipped, and he plunged into the numbing rush of water.

The poet set his feet, took a firmer grip on the younger man's clothes, and hauled his servant free.

"Surely that accident is nothing but an omen," said Biton, as he wrung out the hem of his tunic. His teeth were chattering and he had to stamp his feet to force feeling back into them. "It's certainly a sign that we must turn back, master, and find the daylight again."

Orpheus straightened his servant's garment, laughing gently. "That you are unhurt, Biton, is the most encouraging omen of all."

As they descended, their eyes began to take in enough light to make out ever more easily the path ahead, and the trickling streams that searched their way downward, nearly ice to the touch.

The light that illuminated each turn of the descending passage was more than enough to keep the two from stumbling, but it was an increasingly stale, shale-gray illumination, given off by the cold rock.

Young Biton had never been so uneasy in his life. When at length the passage opened up, an immense cavern rising high above, the poet hurried out into the open void and the servant quailed, "Master, wait for me!"

Before them stretched a river, a current so wide that the opposite bank could barely be observed, a low rim of darkness.

A boat, lopsided and creaking, was making its way in their direction, and Biton began to dread the nature of this vessel even as he felt a shadowy, feathery touch at his arm. Biton sensed an airy grasp take his hand, and a voice making a persistent, nearly silent request.

Fear-sick, the servant spun quickly, and the faint, vaporous entity vanished, only to drift back again, beseeching. "A coin, my lord, if you please, a coin," came the rusty whisper, "so I might find my way across the river."

At the touch of Biton's warm flesh, the phantom presence shrank back once more.

One shade – the remnant of a once living human – lingered closer, circling Biton, rapt with curiosity, it seemed, or intent with menace.

The lad was terrified. He did not even want to breathe the air around such things – they struck him as unclean, maybe even poisonous. Biton felt the strength melt from his knees – it was a struggle to remain upright. He certainly did not trust himself to make a sound.

Noble Orpheus, however, hailed the shades politely, his voice revealing only a hint of his fear. Biton knew his master well enough to admire the show of courage – the poet, too, was no doubt profoundly uneasy in this place.

"The gods' blessing on you all, good friends," said the poet, the silver lyre under his arm reflecting the dull rumor of light.

The shades drew back and fell still, the sound of his polite greeting awakening them perhaps to all the hope and cheer they no longer possessed.

"These are the shades of the impoverished, Biton," Orpheus confided, his voice soft with compassion. "They say that such spirits were too poor to give Charon the ferryman a coin – and so they cannot cross the river Styx."

"Why would they desire," asked Biton, "to cross the black and smelly water?"

Orpheus did not respond at once – he was concerned at the fear in Biton's voice. "They say the dead can rest in peace only near Pluto's palace," the poet explained, putting a protective hand on his companion's shoulder. "Biton – you're shivering!"

"Then let us give them all our gold and silver," said Biton, when he found the power to speak again at all. "Let them cross the river, and let's go back to daylight ourselves." He clutched the poet's arm. "Dear master, we do not belong in this darkness."

"Ferryman, over here," Orpheus was calling.

The boatman poled his lopsided vessel toward them, guiding it with strong, steady plunges of his pole.

"Charon, good master ferryman," Orpheus greeted the boatman – a forced but convincing heartiness as the craft nudged the stony quay. "We have the fee to pay our way across, if you please."

Only then did they see the ferryman's eyes, red-rimmed as though with fire. Charon lifted his pole, dripping with black water, and thrust it at Orpheus's chest, pointing peremptorily with his other hand. *Go back.*

Charon looked hard at Prince Orpheus, and then at the young servant – and gave a wordless hiss of warning.

Biton fainted, falling senseless to the stony quay.

NINETEEN

WHEN BITON was aware of anything, he saw his master kneeling over him.

For an instant the young servant did not know where he was. When he smelled the chill of the river, his heart sank.

"I did not faint, master, despite what you might think," protested Biton. "My feet slipped out from under me, and I found it much wiser to lie down."

Orpheus took Biton's hand. He did not speak for a further moment.

"It was wrong for me to ask you to join me here," said Orpheus at last. "Biton, return to the world of sunlight."

"No, master, please," insisted Biton. "I will prove as sturdy as a donkey, and twice as sure-footed."

"I am requiring you to go back, Biton," said the poet, "and to find provisions for our happy return. You will arrange a merry feast in honor of Eurydice, dear Biton. I give you no choice in the matter."

"I am a worthy servant to you, Prince Orpheus," wailed Biton, torn between duty and relief. "I would go anywhere beside you."

Orpheus put a gentle finger to his servant's lips.

The poet paid the ferryman in gold, far more than the toll of two simple coins a shade would require. Charon looked away, as though loathing the touch of a living mortal, and kept his knobby hand extended until it was full of treasure.

The fine gold reflected no luster in the poor light. The ferryman gave a grunt of assent, at length, and emptied the fistful into a long, weighty purse at his belt.

The poet lifted a hand in farewell, Biton lingering to watch the ferry depart for the opposite bank.

The servant scampered off, on his way back to daylight, and Orpheus felt the damp rise up around him.

Orpheus already missed young Biton badly.

The poet felt all the more alone when the ferryman let his glance flicker over him, his fire-rimmed eyes dismissing the poet, but finding him again with an air of baleful curiosity.

"She's a plucky vessel, is she not?" Orpheus forced himself to say, believing that bright manners were likely to succeed anywhere. The ferry was malformed from an age of working the hard current, so badly warped its deck was uneven, although, Orpheus judged, the craft was surely sturdy enough for another eon of service.

Charon made no response.

Orpheus backed away, toward the center of the broad, ungainly craft as the current lapped up over the ferry's sides, cold and smelling of carrion.

All of this made Orpheus look forward to seeing Eurydice all the more fervently – whatever effort it required. He was certain that soon he must surely free her from this domain.

His determined reverie was shaken by the sound of baying on the far side of the river. Barking and growling echoed fiercely across the sullen current, and it sounded as though three ravening mastiffs were hard on the heels of some quarry.

Surely not, Prince Orpheus tried to console himself. Surely such legendary monsters cannot await me.

The three-headed dog Cerberus snapped and lunged at the approach of the ferry.

The threefold beast grew all the more frenzied as Charon's pole touched the quay, and the ferryman gave a bow and a sweep of his arm, indicating that his passenger was free to make his way.

The monster was restrained by the iron loops of a chain, but the chain was long and did not look strong enough. The three heads erupted from a single, muscular body, and the heads were so ill-tempered that they bit at one another, slavering and disagreeing over which head was the master.

At last the head in the center vanquished its fellows with growls, and turned its fangs in the direction of the poet. Cerberus dragged the iron links with little effort, all the way to their limit, the slavering beast rising up on its hind legs.

However, Charon had allowed Orpheus to disembark farther up the quay than the use-worn stones, shiny with centuries of wear, indicated was customary. The poet was safely ashore.

So perhaps, thought Orpheus, a cheerful tone was not entirely wasted, even along this murky and disagreeable river.

"Thank you, good ferryman," called Orpheus.

Charon offered no courtesy in return, but simply shoved hard against the quay, turning the vessel back into the current.

✻　　✻　　✻

The pathway rose upward from the river, puddles glistening in the glow permeating the darkness.

The source of this illumination was the palace in the distance, its lamps and fires offering dim promise. Shapes flitted through the dark near the towering walls, wings arcing and dodging, and Orpheus could only guess what these flying creatures might be.

Within a few paces, and before Orpheus could allow some tentative hope to kindle in his breast, a fearsome rumble stopped him in his tracks.

It was the grumble of a stone, grinding and bounding down an unseen slope, smashing to a standstill.

Orpheus proceeded along a curve in the path and stopped, unwilling to go farther, taking refuge behind a rocky outcropping.

The sound echoed in the half-dark, the sound of a massive stone being rolled, forced along bedrock, scraping and gritting over an unyielding surface.

Orpheus steeled his nerve, and stepped forward.

TWENTY

A BEARDED FIGURE in a ragged mantle shoved and heaved a massive, irregular boulder up a hill.

The slope was rutted with the passage of this same stone, and the man laboring to work the boulder to the summit of the hill was powerfully built. Even so, he was just able to inch the boulder halfway up the incline when he was forced to fall to one knee, gasping for breath.

Orpheus recognized Sisyphus, damned to this toil by great Jupiter.

As the poet watched, the condemned mortal renewed his effort, powering the boulder upward with sweaty zeal, and with a degree of desperate speed. The boulder was manhandled all the way to the peak of the hill, only to sway unsteadily, and then slowly bound all the way to the base of the incline, back where it had begun.

The figure returned, too, all the way down the slope, trudging heavily but with an air of resignation. The stories Orpheus had heard explained the supposed crime this human being had committed, but the tales did little to make the punishment seem fair. Jupiter had run off with Aegina, daughter of a river god, only to have Sisyphus, a wise and well-liked mortal, disclose to the water deity the place where his daughter had been secreted. For this, Jupiter had decreed an eternal penance: pushing a boulder up a slope that would forever return the stone back to its starting place.

"Sisyphus, may I help you for a while?" asked Orpheus.

The bearded figure gave no sign of having heard, and so the poet asked again.

Sisyphus glanced up from the boulder. "Help me – in what way, traveler?"

"Two of us might make the boulder seem a little lighter."

To the poet's surprise, Sisyphus gave a weary laugh.

"Surely someday," offered Orpheus, "the gods will decide against your punishment, good Sisyphus."

"Do you call this punishment?" asked Sisyphus, putting his shoulder to the massive stone.

"The songs describe you as kind and fair-minded," Orpheus said. "No mortal feels you should suffer in this way."

"What is that frame of silver you carry on your shoulder?" asked Sisyphus, heaving the boulder upward an inch, and then another.

"My lyre – a gift from Apollo," Orpheus answered, feeling how out of place the name of the sunny divinity sounded.

"And you carry it everywhere, do you?"

"Of course – I am happy to," the poet answered in some puzzlement. He introduced himself, and told quickly of his love for Eurydice.

As he spoke, he was startled by a pair of wings that darted through the darkness, followed by another.

The poet ducked his head, and stepped closer to Sisyphus's boulder for brief shelter.

"Those are the Erinyes," said Sisyphus with an air of unconcern. "The Furies – relentless spirits of revenge."

"What do they want of me?" asked Orpheus shakily.

"If you have killed a member of your family," replied Sisyphus, laying both hands on his boulder with something close to affection, "they will see to it that you pay for your crime." Sisyphus leaned forward, heaved, and the boulder rolled slowly upward.

"Dear Sisyphus, do they add to your torment?" asked Orpheus, putting one shoulder into the boulder and helping to shove it higher up the slope.

"Torment!" echoed Sisyphus with a laugh. "Do I seem to be in misery, traveler?"

"Not misery, perhaps, dear Sisyphus," Orpheus was forced to respond after a moment of thought. "But I myself would hate your pointless task."

"The day may come, poet," said Sisyphus with a chuckle, "when you remember me as much like you."

"How am I like you, friend Sisyphus?"

The condemned mortal strained against the great, uneven stone, compelling it upward. "Prince Orpheus," added Sisyphus, through gritted teeth, "someday you may find Apollo's lyre to be heavier than any boulder."

The poet brooded over Sisyphus's remark as he hurried toward his destination.

Another winged shape sliced the air, fluttering phantoms, Furies gathering at the unaccustomed scent of living flesh.

"What breathing wayfarer is that?" came the echoing

question from above in a primordial tongue, the Furies questioning and commenting with each other.

"Oh, let him be a wight who murdered his mother," said one, "or did sunder his father's throat."

Added another, in a tone like rapt anticipation, "So we can tear out his belly and make him writhe."

But another Fury broke off from the rest, and winged her way hard toward the palace.

TWENTY-ONE

ORPHEUS TRAVELED on, toward the still-distant walls.

Feeling hope ebb within his heart, he passed the dimly illuminated shapes of beings in torment.

Tityus, a hoary giant, who long ago tried to violate one of Jupiter's lovers, stretched over several acres of dark ground while vultures plucked at his liver. Tantalus, who once in ages past stole food from Olympus and offered it to mortal men, stood bound forever starving and parched, in a bubbling pool of water.

Orpheus stopped and nearly called out in anguish at the sight of this creature's torture. When the prisoner struggled to take a sip of the water all around, the spring receded, and when he craned his neck to take a bite of the ripe fruit suspended over his head, the nourishment shrank back, just out of reach.

Orpheus hurried on, tears of compassion in his eyes.

Ixion, the first human being to murder another, Orpheus recognized by his particularly agonizing punishment – bound to a wheel that rolled around and around, crushing him but never extinguishing his life.

The poet closed his eyes against the sight, stirred to helpless anger that the powers of this place could be so cruel.

Orpheus's optimism had become increasingly thin, and now as he approached the looming walls of Pluto's palace, he wondered if his quest would, indeed, prove entirely futile. He was unable to keep from hunching his shoulders as yet more Furies swooped down.

The air was even colder now, and its smell was like the wet earth after a heavy paving stone has been lifted – all around, the permeating moisture of minerals and decay.

Beyond the walls and towers lay the plain where the once living slept. A few shades lifted from the expanse and lofted, fragile as breath, above the mute resting place. Never had Orpheus felt so in need of warm-blooded companionship.

As the gates before him opened silently, Orpheus wondered once more if he had been wise in coming here.

He entered the palace, a quaking trespasser in a huge, echoing fortress.

TWENTY-TWO

ONE OF THE Furies trailed behind him, joined by one or two others, not attending him so much as spying over him, a slim, winged form, drifting near and circling the poet wonderingly.

"Don't stay out there in the entryway, Orpheus, son of the immortal muse," intoned a woman's voice from an unseen interior. "Come in here – and quickly."

Nonetheless Orpheus hesitated, tiptoeing forward, across the chilly, polished slabs of the stone floor.

"In here, dear poet," insisted the pleasing voice, which seemed to come from all directions at once.

An inner door fell open with a sound like a sigh, and two figures on thrones sat half shrouded in the lamplight.

Orpheus recognized Persephone from the many poems celebrating her.

She was robed in a green fabric so dark it was nearly black, and her head was encircled with a leafless wreath of ebony stems. She was pale, her lips without color, but her smile and her warm and curious eyes were very much those of a tenderhearted woman as she said, "We welcome you, Prince Orpheus."

A presence sat beside her on a separate throne, a broad-shouldered figure, taller than any human the poet had ever encountered. Only his hands were exposed, large and colorless, adorned with rings of gleaming jet and transparent diamond. This being could only be the lord of the underworld. He was mantled and hooded, his features hidden, and he looked away, pointedly refusing to offer his youthful, mortal visitor so much as a glance.

Orpheus fell to his knees. Even in this citadel, the faraway rumble of Sisyphus's stone could be heard, and the bickering of the distant, hungry vultures.

Being so close to the most profound god touched Orpheus deeply. While uneasy to the point of breathlessness, the poet was filled with reverence. Often known by the more ancient name Hades, Pluto was brother to Neptune and Jupiter, and like them he had lived since the beginning of mortal time.

The uselessness of the poet's pilgrimage here began to dawn all the more deeply upon the bereft traveler.

"How is it, Queen Persephone," he asked in quaking tones, "that you know who I am?"

"My lord and I both extend our greetings to you, Orpheus," replied the queen, with every show of kindness – even as the divinity beside her made neither sound nor gesture. "And we can easily guess the reason you have paid a visit to our realm." She answered his query only then by adding, "Do you think that at least one of the timeless Furies could not recognize the grandson of Jupiter?"

Orpheus had all but lost the gift of speech, his last hope vanishing. It was with effort that he recalled his habitual good manners. He climbed to his feet as he found the power to say, "All the creatures of daylight, Queen Persephone, honor you." He hastened to add, "And we honor your lord, too."

This last remark was little more than a weak courtesy – and a vain attempt to flatter. In truth, men and women never did raise a temple to Hades, or hold even the briefest festival in his name. Of all the gods he was the one thought to be the least concerned with human beings and their pleasures, not evil in character so much as abysmally indifferent. Within his peaked hood his features were veiled, and this figure turned resolutely away from his visitor.

"I don't forget what it was like to be a mortal woman," Persephone was saying, her voice gentle and low, but carrying into the recesses of this palace, and softly echoing. "I remember the sun on my shoulders, and how it warmed my hair." She laughed at this memory, as though surprised at it, and touched the naked wreath around her head.

The queen straightened on her throne, like a woman stirring herself to more serious and present matters. She leveled her gaze at the young poet. "But we anticipate your reason for journeying so far into our world, and we must warn you, good Orpheus – what you want is impossible."

TWENTY-THREE

"HOW CAN YOU steal the request from my lips?" Orpheus found the power to protest.

"We respect your steadfast love, Prince Orpheus," she responded, "but no human soul can be returned to life once it sleeps in our kingdom. Not even someone as noble-natured and beloved as your Eurydice."

Hearing the name of his bride spoken in this cold palace gave

Orpheus such pain, and filled him with such longing, that he struggled to keep from groaning aloud.

"Queen Persephone," said the poet, his voice hoarse with feeling, "I have come to sing for you." Orpheus despaired now that any poetry could stir compassion from such a place, but he would not depart without lifting his voice.

"Will you play us a tune," asked Persephone, with something very much like hope, "on that gift from Apollo?"

Orpheus cradled the lyre. Even here in this chill, the silver frame was warm beneath his touch.

"I pray that I may," Orpheus managed to respond.

Persephone clasped her hands thoughtfully, as though weighing the consequences of music in such a place. She turned to look at her husband, but Lord Hades continued to give no sign that he was aware of their guest.

"You may sing for us, Orpheus," said Queen Persephone at last, "and play Apollo's lyre – but only with my lord's permission."

She turned her head and waited for the grand, hooded figure beside her to make a sound. The god showed no sign of having heard – except to turn, almost imperceptibly, even farther away.

Persephone waited for the immortal husband to show some sign of permission, but at last she turned to Orpheus and parted her hands.

There is nothing I can do.

Orpheus touched the strings, accidentally, as he turned away from the king and queen, ready to set down the silver instrument. This grazing touch, a chance chord, made such a sweet stir in this shadowy chamber that he could not keep his hand from plucking the chord again – a beautiful sound.

> *The shadow of your hand,*
> *Eurydice,*
> *among the shadows of the birds*
> *on a summer morning.*

Orpheus lifted this quiet verse to the murmur of the lyre.

He had not intended to sing at all, and indeed his voice was barely above a whisper. But this soft fragment of song, created in the moment, was enough to cause a drifting shape to scurry toward him, eyes sharp, joined at once by another, the Furies gathering, so fierce with curiosity that Orpheus nearly dropped his lyre.

He touched the strings again.

> *I stir,*
> *Eurydice,*
> *thinking you have touched me –*
> *forgetting.*

The Furies hurried into a circle around him, winged apparitions like winged women, now that the poet beheld them clearly. In an uncanny way, they possessed a stark beauty. Their black eyes were hungry, silently insisting to Orpheus, *Sing, sing.*

Their fierce attention prompted the poet to raise his voice, as his fingers remembered the chords he had learned from the lord of daylight.

The poet sang of Eurydice, and of his love. He offered verses that he would later find lost to memory.

When he was done, he stood with the lyre still vibrating from the last chord, and became aware again of the Furies around him, and the now-tearful eyes of Queen Persephone.

I came to sing poetry, thought Orpheus, and so I have.

He was resigned, in his sadness, to whatever requirements the powers of this kingdom might command. But Orpheus realized then what a deep silence now surrounded the palace.

The rumble of Sisyphus's boulder, the snapping squabble of the vultures had ceased. In the corridors, the shade of a human ghost, joined by several others, stood rapt to catch the last echoes of music that even then reverberated through the underworld.

At last the silence was complete, and Persephone turned and put a slender hand on the forearm of her husband – just once, a single touch.

For a long while nothing moved. No Fury made an utterance,

and no shade drifted back to its resting place. The impassive Hades remained as he had been, and made no sound.

But then he moved, very slowly.

The veiled shape of Hades shifted on his throne, just slightly, turning back toward Persephone. The great figure lifted a single, blackly jeweled finger, and like a monarch that did nothing in haste, he leaned heavily toward the queen.

The veil fluttered softly before his lips.

The whisper he gave was wordless to Orpheus's ears, but Persephone caught its meaning.

She put her hands together, a gesture of relief and quiet thanksgiving.

"You may take Eurydice back into the daylight," said Persephone, a thrill in her voice.

Orpheus was unable to respond at first – hopeful anticipation was equally mingled with disbelief in the poet's heart.

"You may return her to life," said Persephone with a smile. But then she lifted a hand, a warning gesture. "But there is one condition you must observe without fail, Prince Orpheus."

"I will do anything," responded Orpheus. "What task must I perform to bring Eurydice to the world of the living?"

TWENTY-FOUR

"MY LORD and husband decrees that you may return Eurydice to the living, Prince Orpheus," said Persephone with a pensive smile, "but on one very firm and unwavering condition."

"I will pay any price," said Orpheus excitedly.

She silenced him, lifting a hand. "On the journey," she continued, "you must not turn back to look at her — not even once."

The poet considered. This would certainly be a relatively easy restriction to fulfill, he thought. "There is no additional condition?"

"You must not look upon her for a single moment, Orpheus," Persephone insisted earnestly, "once you have departed from this palace. Do you understand?"

"Indeed I do," responded the poet with increasing enthusiasm.

"There will be no second opportunity," said Persephone. "If you lose her again, Prince Orpheus, she will be lost forever."

Orpheus gave an excited laugh, his pulse racing.

"I promise," the poet said, "that I will lead the way – and not look back until we emerge from this domain." The young mortal could not add another word, so great was his excitement – and his growing faith that he was close to seeing Eurydice again.

"I shall call for her, then," said Persephone in a low voice, half question, half promise.

"Please, great queen," Orpheus managed to say, "send for my beloved."

Persephone smiled, closed her eyes, and whispered, "Eurydice!"

A soft wind took up the syllables, the name cascading through the corridors of the palace, out into the muted plain beyond. The gathered Furies joined in, a chorus of half-voiced calls.

Eurydice!

Twenty-Five

Nothing Happened.

For a long, seemingly endless moment there was no running figure, no breathless laugh, no longed-for voice calling his name. Orpheus began to dread that the promise would be mocked with failure – or, even worse, that some dim, tattered shade would appear, not at all like a living woman.

Nothing. There was no greeting cry, no loving smile. Orpheus was embittered with his own, tantalizing hope.

Until he heard a footfall.

A shuffling, limping approach.

Eurydice groped her way, her stride still stricken by the serpent's bite, into the shadowy light of the great hall.

While the poet was ecstatic at the sight of her, he felt remorse, too, at the sight of her suffering.

"Are you in pain, Eurydice?" he asked, reaching out – and nearly succeeding in touching her.

Yes, she would have said, if she had found the power to speak at that moment. And yet this was not true pain, Eurydice knew. The real agony had been in those last moments, the viper's fangs hooked deep into her foot, all the way to the bone, while the venom shriveled her heart.

Eurydice tentatively, and with effort, made sense of what was happening to her. She had no reason to easily trust her senses. Death had been like peaceful sleep, dreamless and without pain. Suddenly called again to awareness, she did not want to give herself too freely to happiness – all this might prove to be a fugitive vision. Could it be that Orpheus had died, too, and joined her here as a faded soul?

The twin fang punctures in her ankle were bleeding again. She trembled, her heart beating unsteadily, breath haltingly expanding and contracting in her cold lungs. Certainly, she told herself, her beloved looked like a living human being. Orpheus had color in his cheeks, and vitality in his eyes.

She was eager to touch the poet, hold him, and yet she faltered, fearful of the mantled, veiled figure on the throne beside smiling, pale-featured Persephone.

Increasingly joyful as she was, she had been a king's daughter, accustomed to complex agreements and diplomatic turnabouts. She surmised that some dread contract had been struck, one that must be strictly observed.

For this reason, as she put her cold hand into Orpheus's warm grasp at last, she said, "My love, what promises have you given to bring me forth?"

Her voice was shaky, merely a torn whisper, but the son of Calliope understood her well. Orpheus took both her icy hands, and laughed, gathering her into his arms – gently, as though he could injure her too easily. Her flesh remained cold – but warmer by the moment.

He described the simple condition.

How fast his heart was beating, she thought, her own pulse stirring and gradually keeping its pace.

"That's the only vow you have made?" she queried when she had heard everything. "That you not look back to see me?"

She put her hand on his face, and ran her fingertips over his features. For the first time she felt the spark of deliverance.

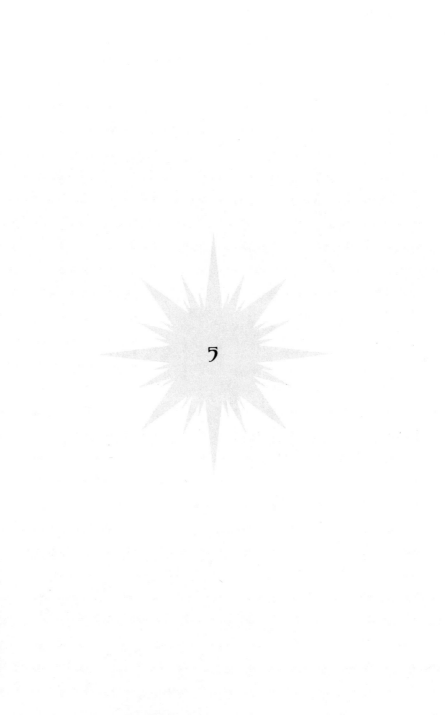

5

TWENTY-SIX

ORPHEUS AND EURYDICE made all possible haste.

The two lovers were in too great a hurry to spare a moment to watch the rumbling progress of Sisyphus's boulder, commencing once again on its relentless course.

They approached the river Styx breathlessly, and waited there as the lopsided ferry surged toward them, the three-headed beast on the riverbank growling and snapping, restrained by its chain.

Charon was silent, but gave the poet a meaningful look and patted his heavy purse as though to say, *You've paid enough already.*

Perhaps eager to rid the dark realm of two living mortals, the ferryman plunged his pole at once into the water. They crossed the foul-smelling river quickly, and soon Orpheus felt the opposite quay beneath his feet.

"Don't!" gasped Eurydice as Orpheus nearly turned back to help her disembark from the lopsided ferry.

The young poet shook himself, and gave an embarrassed — and startled — laugh.

He was aching for another sight of her — and shocked to find how hard it might be to fulfill the simple, stark condition.

Orpheus crept along the path, keeping his own progress slow, and reaching back often to take her hand.

Even so, at times she fell behind, and the poet had to pause and listen carefully to catch the whisper of her footsteps. Reassured by her approaching, limping footfall, he would hurry ahead — only to stop and hold his breath as her progress was too far in the distance to make an audible sound. Perhaps she has lost the way, he thought several times, only to grow weak with relief as her steps made their way upward, closer and closer.

She had many questions — about the well-being of her father,

her brother, and all her many friends in the kingdom. Orpheus was delighted to tell her every detail as they journeyed upward, reassured that the mourning he described would soon be swept away by joyful life. When he got too far ahead once more, he called back to her and she answered, "I'm coming, Orpheus," laughing breathlessly, as though her injury was a minor hindrance, nothing more.

And as she climbed upward, she was growing stronger – the poet could hear it in her voice and feel it in the increasingly assertive grasp she offered him.

It was true that the route was more rough and even more dangerous than Orpheus had recalled, the upward effort more difficult than the descent. For this reason the poet walked increasingly well ahead at times, sweeping sharp pebbles from the path with eager hands.

The music of water, trickling down from above, reached his ears. The snaking roots of trees speared downward, through cracks in the rocks, and lichen splashed the stone walls. Just when Orpheus sniffed the first trace of daylight air, he stumbled, and put out a hand to the rocky wall to keep from falling to the stony floor.

The trail crumbled, and broke away beneath his feet, the rocky shelf falling off into the dark. But only at the sound of Eurydice's warning gasp did the poet realize that he had once again nearly turned back.

"It isn't far now," he said, his voice broken with anguish at the fatal blunder he had almost committed.

Not far – his pulse hammered out the message.

We are almost there.

TWENTY-SEVEN

AT LAST ORPHEUS stood beside the hard-gushing stream where Biton had slipped during the descent – it seemed so long ago.

"Wait, Eurydice," he cautioned her without turning back. "I'll make sure the footing is sound."

He stepped into the numbing water, alarmed at the loose stones that quaked and churned, nearly causing him to fall.

He struggled through the icy torrent.

And then he waited as Eurydice paused at the far bank of the stream. He continued to linger where he was, turned resolutely away from her, as she haltingly waded forward. He heard her shudder at the cold, and sensed her reaching for his hand.

He continued to turn deliberately away from her, and at the same time he reached back. He stretched his hand all the way, as far as he could, praying that soon he would feel her touch.

It did not come.

She's fallen.

She's helpless.

Surely, he thought, that splashing is the sound of her trying to keep from drowning. Just one look, he thought. An instant glimpse would not really count against me – would it?

Of course not. I'll take one quick glance, nothing more.

He got ready to take just one peek. Just one, to prevent her from drowning.

Eurydice screamed.

She had been balancing, step by step, across the uneven streambed, and making good progress – but slow. Her injury no longer hurt at all, and she was filled with ever-increasing hope. Wasn't that vague glow from far above the promise of daylight?

She was more than halfway across the rushing water when Orpheus turned back and met her eyes.

Her lungs shrank again, and her blood ceased to pulse.

Her heart contracted to a cold fist in her breast and her cry became a rattle. All the life that had returned to her body, giving it weight and color, ebbed away in moments, sinews dissolving, bone turning to smoke, a living woman becoming a shade again, and dissolving as she silently shrilled his name.

TWENTY-EIGHT

BITON FOUND Orpheus in the sunlight the next day, sitting on the shore.

The youth led a sure-footed donkey burdened with ripe dates and sesame cakes, red wine and fresh-baked loaves – the makings of a welcome feast for Orpheus and his rescued bride.

The poet spoke no word, and gave no sign of hearing Biton's questions. The youthful servant could only spread a blanket, prepare a meal, and taste some of it encouragingly. And then, when his master made no move to eat, Biton packed the rest of it away.

The young servant could not imagine what his master had seen or suffered. Biton knew it was a selfish, small thing to take delight in, but he was glad to have his master back safe.

That was enough to make Biton thankful, but as the days went on, the servant grew increasingly concerned for the princely poet.

Biton had observed his master's deep mourning before, but nothing like this. The poet was not bereaved so much as void, lost to nearly every sound and sight around him. For days Orpheus did not eat, and he said nothing, watching the waves break and the foam sink into the rocky shore.

Biton held a cup of weak wine to his master's lips, and the poet – his face a silent mask of sorrow – took in just enough to stay alive. His lyre rested against a stone untouched as Orpheus watched the round sun set and the stars rise. How many days were spent like this Biton would never be able to guess, but it was at dawn when at last he saw his master standing, letting the salt water lap at his ankles.

Orpheus gestured out to sea, indicating a vessel beyond the waves, drawing in its sail.

Biton recognized the *Actis* even though her canvas was new and dazzling white. Red-haired Captain Idas waved from the bow.

"We were worried about you," called the seaman. "How are you faring?"

The poet waded toward the ship, out into the easy surf, leaving the lyre of Apollo on the shore.

Biton gave a cry of alarm. He hurried to rescue the instrument from the sand. It remained heavy and silent in the youth's grasp as he carried it out to the newly painted vessel and her friendly crew.

Days later the *Actis* delivered the poet and his servant to the island of Delos, a wooded, prosperous island with a wide, shallow harbor of industrious net weavers and sturdy fishing vessels.

Biton and the captain selected the destination. Orpheus had said nothing regarding where he wished to journey, neither to the captain nor to any of the crew, and Biton could offer little to enlighten them.

"The little isle is a sunny place, with a balmy wind," Captain Idas suggested. "And the priests of the famous temple of Apollo there will be sure to honor your master."

The poet took no interest in the smiles of the fisherfolk, however, nor the delegation of white-haired temple priests bringing fig cakes and berry wine – a specialty of the island – to express their welcome to the poet.

"My master is bereaved," explained Biton simply.

Every time a request arrived for the renowned singer to join the villagers in a celebration of a recent birth, or to sing a song of blessing for a departing fishing fleet, the answer was the same.

Every day Biton made sure that his master's tunic was fresh, and his hair groomed. As the weeks passed, however, the servant was increasingly lonely for stories or poems – for any sort of conversation at all. And Biton felt curious, too – altogether too curious to keep silent much longer.

What had happened across the black river Styx, he wondered, in the palace of Hades?

One evening Biton cut a finger on the scales of a large red fish, a gift from the villagers. The scaly prize was nearly as big as Biton himself, and the servant had been cleaning the giant, when blood welled on his finger.

To his surprise, Orpheus was at his side in an instant, after a month of stony torpor, dabbing at the injury with a bit of linen.

"Be careful, Biton," said Orpheus, wrapping the finger with a bandage, the first words he had uttered in an age.

The poet dressed Biton's cut with care the next morning, talking haltingly all the while, telling of his journey to Hades' palace.

"Two times, Biton," he said, anguish in his voice, "my beautiful Eurydice was taken from me."

The poet would say nothing more.

"Sing me a song about her," suggested Biton, tears in his own eyes. "Make up a poem about lovely Eurydice, master. Please, to ease our sorrow – both yours and mine."

But Orpheus turned away from the sight of his lyre.

The thought of poetry was so much long-cold ash to him, and the memory of song was bitter. Orpheus did not foresee his hands ever plucking music again, and could not imagine spinning a verse as long as he might live.

Immortal Hades knew that I would turn back, thought Orpheus bitterly. And so did the lovely Queen Persephone.

The condition set forth by her enigmatic husband was little more than a snare, sure to trap Eurydice, and send me into daylight alone.

TWENTY-NINE

WHEN THE SUN was high one late-summer day, a visitor
arrived.

He was a priest from the temple of Apollo, a now familiar,
ruddy-featured man. He was in a hurry, sweating and breathing
hard, and this time brought a goatskin of berry wine and a woven
sack of fresh, sun-bright apples.

He ducked into the shadowy entryway of Orpheus's dwelling,

and explained to Biton. "The villagers have a heartfelt request," said the priest, "for your master's aid."

Biton sighed. "He never departs these walls."

"If you could bring yourself to ask, most earnestly, dear Biton," said the good-natured priest, concern in his eyes. "There has been a fearsome accident, and we need the prince's help."

Orpheus was sitting indoors, listening to the energetic bickering of the birds in the eaves over his head. It had been a long time since he had taken any pleasure in the sound, and just now, for the first time in months, he had to admit that the feathered creatures made a pretty chatter.

"Young Norax, son of a tinsmith, fell off a roof, master," Biton said, repeating the priest's tidings to Orpheus. "He was trying to retrieve a ball from a courtyard game, and he slipped off and struck his head." The servant did not know how else to put it. "The temple prayers have not been heeded by the gods, and now the village hopes your songs might awaken the boy to life."

"It troubles me to hear this news," said Orpheus.

But of course I can do nothing, he nearly added.

The poet listened to the sparrows and the doves that nested in the roof. He thought, how much like human speech – the warmhearted chatter of wharf and market – their sounds were.

I'm here, the birds said to each other.

I live, I live, they announced with mindless energy, little feathered knots of vitality while the lovely Eurydice slept.

But was that all they said?

Perhaps you should, perhaps you should.

He rose to his feet, tentatively, and found his way out of the cool interior, standing under the bright sun.

He had been indoors too long, he thought. The songbirds were beginning to speak Greek.

"The day is warm," said Orpheus, taking a few experimental steps across the stone-strewn ground, taking pleasure in the sound of the pebbles under his sandals. "And the sky is –"

What word could describe such a sky. *Empty? Blue? Full of promise?* Words were not equal to such an expanse of heaven.

Or were they?

"Is it true, Prince Orpheus," the suntanned priest was asking excitedly, "that divine Apollo once spoke with you?"

"The blessings of the gods on you, good priest," said Orpheus, remembering his customary, if long-neglected, courtesy.

The poet took a deep breath, not wanting to speak further of divine things just now. He felt unsteady from his long inactivity, and amazed at the heady perfume of sea air.

Orpheus glanced upward once more, at the dazzling source of

daylight high above. Sometimes it was said that Apollo mourned with mortals when they were sad, and did what he could to lessen human grief.

If this happened to be true, thought Orpheus, I have seen no recent sign of it. The god of daylight, who had once allowed his mortal son to scorch the world with his wayward chariot, remained largely remote and heedless. At least, that was how it seemed to the poet now.

"The lord of daylight walked with me, that's a fact," he told the eager priest. "One timeless, wonderful day – long ago."

"And is it true what they say, Prince?" persisted the priest, almost too excited to complete his question. "That the divine Apollo endowed you with a finely wrought silver lyre?"

Biton's cry stopped Orpheus, and he turned back.

The young servant ran, carrying the silver instrument, the frame and strings bright in the sunlight. "Master, I expected the metal to be tarnished, after all these months," exclaimed Biton. "But look – how beautiful it is, after all this time!"

Orpheus took the instrument reluctantly into his grasp. But then he cradled it with less hesitation, surprised at how comfortably it settled into his arms.

"The legends," said the priest, rapture in his eyes, "report that your lyre never tarnishes, and never needs to be tuned."

"That's all true," the poet heard himself say. He returned the lyre to his servant's arms. "But my fingers will have grown clumsy – I have not plucked a single chord for many months."

But the priest did not hear this – he hurried on ahead, into the village.

THIRTY

THE GRATEFUL and excited crowd parted as Orpheus and Biton hastened toward the dwelling place of the injured child.

The young boy lay senseless, his mother gently soothing his forehead with a soft cloth, his father stirring a brazier of healing herbs.

The poet knelt beside the sickbed without speaking. Young Norax was much closer to death than Orpheus had expected, his breath slow and shallow, eyelids parted but his eyes unseeing.

This troubled the poet very much.

Orpheus had thought that one of the jolly old verses, unaccompanied by the lyre – perhaps one of the many stories of goat-footed Pan and his adventures – would cheer an injured boy. However, this patient was beyond such childish ditties. The physician in the corner gave Orpheus a shrug: *What more can I do?*

The poet could not bear to see the child so close to death, or the parents so cruelly caught between hope and anguish. Remembering all the other times the lyre and fervent poetry had shown power, Orpheus turned solemnly to Biton.

The poet did not have to speak.

Biton presented the bright-framed lyre.

And the servant was not alone in holding his breath, leaning forward to catch the first sound.

It has been long, thought Orpheus, since I have tried to play.

Too long, and my heart is far too heavy, and surely the skill has faded from my fingers.

He touched the instrument gently, nonetheless, feeling the familiar strings vibrant and supple beneath his trembling fingers.

He nearly dropped the lyre, shocked at what he heard.

7

THIRTY-ONE

THE SOUND that lifted upward from the lyre was not a mere musical note, soft but sustained.

It was the unmistakable whisper, *"Orpheus!"*

There could be no doubt.

It was the voice of Eurydice.

Orpheus did not dare to touch the strings again, certain, despite the evidence of his own hearing, that he was being tricked by some hard-hearted prankster. He glanced around at the expectant faces of parents and friends, ready to burst out accusingly, *Which of you is cruel and spiteful enough to taunt me?*

Biton's innocently wondering smile, and the rapt, eager features of the assembled family, answered Orpheus's silent question.

I'll try that note again, he thought.

In a moment – when I've recovered my senses.

When he could not hesitate any longer, he stretched his fingers again, and it seemed that the strings moved, seeking his hand more eagerly than ever before.

The poet plucked a new chord, and he heard her again: *"Orpheus, sing with me!"*

He nearly stood upright, and almost let the lyre fall once more – but he remained seated, stunned into new silence.

The others in the room waited, anticipation in their eyes, unaware of the presence that resounded in the sickroom only in the poet's ears.

Only Orpheus could hear her voice, it seemed. He ran his finger along a string, and there she was again, singing the syllables of his name.

Orpheus found new music, plucking tenderly, listening with increasing joy to the sound of Eurydice the way he had first heard her, bathing in the woods, lifting her voice in praise of the divine Juno.

As he played, her voice surrounded him, a living presence.
And, breathlessly at first, so Orpheus lifted his voice with hers.

What is day,
what is night,
your footstep so close.

Young Norax stirred on his sickbed, blinking. He rose to one elbow, his lips parted, caught by the poem.

The injured boy sat up, gazing at the source of the music, Orpheus and the shining lyre. Norax smiled, happy but confused at the cries of gratitude as his parents knelt beside his sickbed, and gathered him into their arms.

From that day, and throughout the era of Orpheus's journeys that followed, into distant lands, each time he placed his hand on the lyre, he heard the voice of Eurydice.

And every day of the poet's life he sang with her.

AUTHOR'J NOTE

While I create my own stories based on the myths portrayed by the Latin poet Ovid, his magnificent poem *The Metamorphoses* remains one of the inspirations for my own writings about the classical era.

For this reason, I use the Roman names for the gods and goddesses. Minerva is not entirely the same goddess as Athena, and Jupiter is not exactly the same as Zeus. However, I have decided to continue to follow Ovid's names for the divinities in the interest of consistency, and out of respect for that great poet and the world he brought to life.